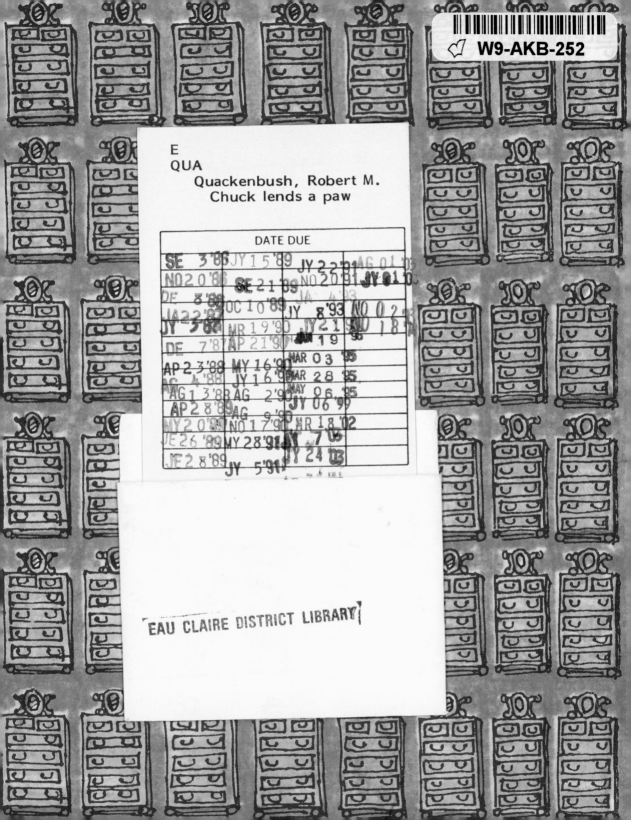

W9-AKB-252

E
QUA
 Quackenbush, Robert M.
 Chuck lends a paw

CHUCK LENDS A PAW

by Robert Quackenbush

CLARION BOOKS
TICKNOR & FIELDS: A HOUGHTON MIFFLIN COMPANY
NEW YORK

Clarion Books
Ticknor & Fields, a Houghton Mifflin Company
Copyright © 1986 by Robert Quackenbush

Library of Congress Cataloging in Publication Data

Quackenbush, Robert M.
Chuck lends a paw.
Summary: Chuck Mouse helps his friend, Maxine, move
a tall chest of drawers with disastrous results.
[1. Mice—Fiction. 2. Friendship—Fiction] I. Title.
PZ7.Q16Ch 1986   [E]   85-14917
ISBN 0-89919-363-3

Y 10 9 8 7 6 5 4 3 2 1

For Piet

Chuck Mouse got a call
from his friend, Maxine.
She told him that she had
just moved to a new house.
"But the movers left a
chest on the porch of
my old house," said Maxine.
"Could you bring it to my
front door in your pick-up
truck, Chuck? The address
is 1033 River Drive."

Chuck said he would be
glad to lend a paw.
He drove his pick-up
to Maxine's old house.
He got the chest and
took it to 1033 River Drive.
But when he got there he saw
that Maxine's new house
was on the top of a hill.
He would have to climb
a lot of steps to deliver
the chest.

Chuck took the chest
off the truck and wheeled
it over to the steps.
He began pushing and
pulling the chest up
one step at a time.

Halfway up the steps,
the chest began to topple.
In a flash, Chuck jumped
in front of it.
But he couldn't stop
the chest from falling.

Crash!
Down came the chest
on top of poor Chuck.

Chuck had to think of
a new way to get the
chest up the steps.
He saw some boards
lying on the sidewalk.
Carefully, he lined up
the boards on the steps.
Then he wheeled the chest
onto the boards and
began to push.

Up, up the boards
went the chest.
Just as Chuck reached
the top step, the
boards began to slide.
So did the chest!
So did Chuck!

Down the steps at full speed
came the boards, the chest,
and Chuck.
On the way, one of the
boards slammed into
Maxine's lawn sprinkler
and broke it!

Then the boards and Chuck
bumped into Maxine's trash cans
and knocked them over.
Slam! Bang!
Trash was scattered
everywhere!

Finally the chest plowed
into a fire hydrant
and broke that!
Poor, poor Chuck.
What a mess he had caused!

As if that weren't
enough, along came
a policeman.
He gave Chuck a ticket
for creating a disturbance,
destroying public property,
littering,
and much, much more.

After that, there was
only one thing left
for Chuck to do.
He got a screwdriver
from his truck and proceeded
to take the chest apart.
Then he began carrying
it up the steps a few
pieces at a time.

Just as Chuck got
the last pieces to the house,
Maxine came around the side.
"Oh, there you are, Chuck,"
she said. "I've been
looking for you."
She saw the pieces of
chest lying on the ground.
"What happened!" she cried.

"Don't worry, Maxine,"
said Chuck
"I can fix the chest.
It was the only way
I could get it up the steps.
But let me tell you
about something else
that happened.
Something much worse…"
"Wait, Chuck," said Maxine.
"Did you say steps?"
"Yes—the steps to your
front door," Chuck replied.

"But, Chuck," said Maxine,
"this isn't the front door.
It's the back. You could have
driven right up to the front."

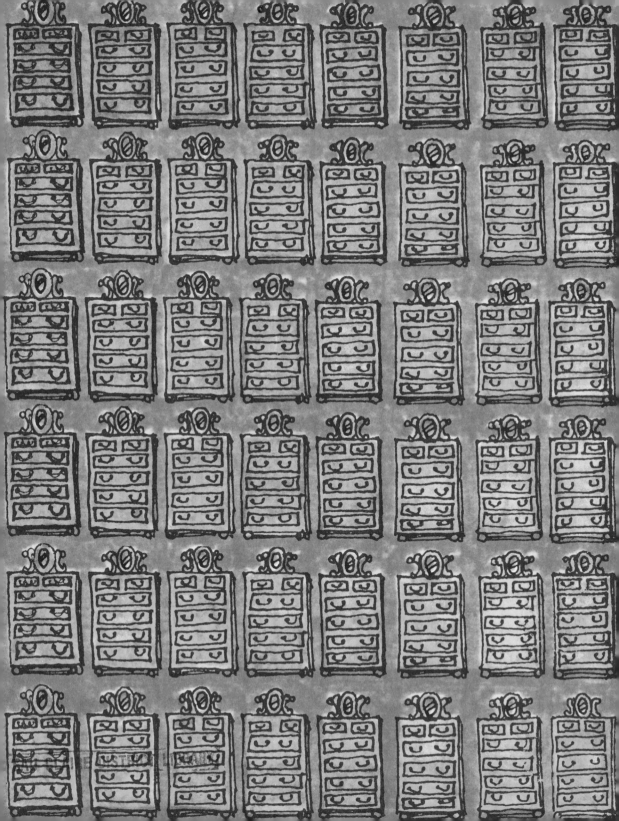